Boxcar Children Mysteries

THE BOXCAR CHILDREN
SURPRISE ISLAND
THE YELLOW HOUSE MYSTERY
MYSTERY RANCH
MIKE'S MYSTERY
BLUE BAY MYSTERY
THE WOODSHED MYSTERY
THE LIGHTHOUSE MYSTERY
MOUNTAIN TOP MYSTERY
SCHOOLHOUSE MYSTERY
CABOOSE MYSTERY
HOUSEBOAT MYSTERY
SNOWBOUND MYSTERY
TREE HOUSE MYSTERY
BICYCLE MYSTERY
MYSTERY IN THE SAND
MYSTERY BEHIND THE WALL
BUS STATION MYSTERY
BENNY UNCOVERS A MYSTERY
THE HAUNTED CABIN MYSTERY
THE DESERTED LIBRARY MYSTERY
THE ANIMAL SHELTER MYSTERY

THE ANIMAL SHELTER MYSTERY

created by
GERTRUDE CHANDLER WARNER

Illustrated by Charles Tang

SCHOLASTIC INC.
New York Toronto London Auckland Sydney

12 11 10 9 8 7 6 5 4 3   1 2 3 4 5 6/9

Printed in the U.S.A.   28

First Scholastic printing, November 1991

Contents

CHAPTER 1

A Thump at the Window

Dinner at the Aldens' ended with the sound of a growl. Henry, Jessie, Violet, and Grandfather Alden, too, all turned to look at Watch.

"What's the matter, Watch?" Jessie asked the family dog.

"Did you hear that fat raccoon again?" Violet wanted to know.

"Or maybe a skunk, boy?" Henry asked.

Watch answered all these questions with another growl. This surprised everyone at the dinner table but Benny. He was too busy spooning up his blueberries and vanilla ice cream to pay any attention to Watch.

Something hit the screen, and Watch's growl turned into a real bark. Something — or someone — was at the porch window, trying to get in!

"I'll go out back and check," Henry said.

Now Benny dropped his spoon into the bowl. He ran out to the porch with everyone else. "Maybe it's a prowler," he said.

"Oh!" Violet cried out suddenly. "Something just brushed against my legs."

Jessie stooped down. "Why, look," she said. "It's not a prowler at all. It's a little calico cat."

"So this ball of fur was trying to get into our house?" Mr. Alden asked. He laughed as an orange, gray, and white cat circled through everyone's legs.

Violet picked up the cat. "I think she's lost, poor thing."

"And hungry," Benny added. He quickly ran into the dining room and came back with his ice-cream bowl.

"She *is* hungry," Jessie said. "Look how

fast she's lapping up Benny's dessert."

In no time at all Benny's bowl was licked clean.

Mr. Alden smiled. His grandchildren had adopted many pets since the old boxcar days when Watch first showed up to protect them. Of course, the Aldens didn't need much protection anymore. After their parents died, their grandfather had found them living in a boxcar and brought them home to his big safe house.

"Listen!" Jessie said when the cat finished her dinner. "She's purring."

"Sounds like she's got a little radio in there," Benny said, laughing. "For such a small cat, she sure has a big purr."

"How do you know she's a *she*?" Henry asked. "Maybe she's a *he*."

"Dr. Scott, the animal doctor, told me calico cats are always girl cats," Violet explained.

Though Violet was only ten, her family knew she must be right. The Aldens were all working as volunteers at the Greenfield Animal Shelter this summer, but Violet was

Dr. Scott's special helper. No one was gentler than Violet when it came to soothing scared animals or fixing their hurts.

"Well, let's see if this girl cat has a name," Mr. Alden said. "There's some sort of tag on her collar."

Jessie took a look. "It's a locket. Here, Violet, you open it. It's too small for my fingers."

Violet's delicate fingers opened the locket with no trouble at all. "Why, look, there's a message inside!" she cried. A folded piece of paper fell out of the locket.

Benny got to it first. He brushed back his hair from his eyes. "I'll read it," he said. "Now that I'm six, I know how to read."

And so he did . . . with some help from Jessie.

> *My name is Patches. My owner can no longer take care of me. I know you children will give me a good home.*

"Then she's not *really* lost," Jessie said. "Somebody left her here on purpose,"

Henry agreed. "But why? And why did they bring her to our house?"

"Maybe the person wanted *this* home," Benny said. "Not just any old place, but Grandfather's house, with a big porch, and a boxcar in the backyard, and blueberries and ice cream, and everything just right."

Mr. Alden smiled. He was happy to hear Benny say this. His grandson was right. Anyone who wanted a good home couldn't do any better than the Alden place.

Jessie looked puzzled. She twisted her braid around her finger. "Patches is such a healthy and friendly cat. Her owners must have taken very good care of her. Why would they give her away?"

"We should try to find out who her owners are," Violet said. "And what their reason was for giving her to us."

"I wish we could keep this cat," Benny said. "She likes us. Can we keep her just for tonight? Please?"

"Sure thing, Benny," Henry said. He gave his little brother a pat on the head. "I guess she can sleep in one of our rooms."

Just then, Watch barked.

"Patches can't sleep inside," Jessie said. "We have to be careful of Watch's feelings. Patches can stay on the screened porch. It's a lovely summer night. We'll leave a small light on to keep her company."

Violet added, "We can make up a small bed for her out there in Benny's red wagon."

"With a soft mattress," Jessie said. She came back out to the porch carrying a flannel-covered pillow. She tucked it in the wagon and tried to coax Patches to climb up. But the little cat wasn't interested.

"She's nervous," Violet said. "I know what she needs." She whispered something in Mr. Alden's ear, then ran upstairs. When she came down again, she was carrying something lumpy wrapped in an old towel. She laid the lump carefully on the pillow in Benny's wagon. "There you go," she said. She lifted the cat and placed her on the pillow.

The cat sniffed the lump, walked in a circle around the pillow, then curled up.

"What did you put there, Violet?" Benny asked.

"It's Grandfather's big black alarm clock. The ticking will make Patches think of her mother's heartbeat. That will help her sleep," Violet explained.

"Well, what do you know!" Henry said. "Look at that."

Everyone stared at Patches. She was practically asleep already!

"I don't know who or why somebody left her here, but they certainly picked the right place," Mr. Alden said. He left on the porch light but locked the screen door. "Time for all of us to get to sleep, too."

Jessie coaxed Benny into the house. "We'll have to get up early if we're going to look for this cat's owner before we go to the animal shelter. If everyone helps me in the morning on my newspaper route, we'll have time to talk to people along the way. Maybe someone will know where Patches came from."

Everyone looked back once more to check on their calico guest. Cuddled in Benny's wagon, the cat looked right at home. But how had she gotten here? The Aldens meant to find out.

CHAPTER 2

Missing Person

The Aldens had their own alarm clock to wake them up every day. With the first ray of light, Watch stood by Jessie's bed and pushed her with his nose. Then he visited Henry and Violet and did the same thing.

Benny needed something different to wake up. Watch tugged at the blankets until Benny opened his eyes.

"It's still dark out," Benny told the dog. He pulled the covers over his head.

Watch pulled them down again.

"Okay, boy, okay. I'll *get* up. But that doesn't mean I'll *wake* up."

Benny was wrong. Suddenly he remembered what was special about today. Wide awake now, he ran downstairs and rushed out to the porch. Too late. Violet, Jessie, and Henry were already there, feeding Patches bits of scrambled eggs.

"Is that my breakfast?" Benny cried.

Henry laughed. "Don't worry, there's plenty left in the kitchen."

"Boy, for such a small cat, she sure eats a lot," Benny told the housekeeper, Mrs. McGregor, when he got to the kitchen.

Mrs. McGregor couldn't help laughing. "And for such a small boy, *you* sure eat a lot!"

Benny helped himself to a heap of scrambled eggs with cheddar cheese, and two pieces of toast with peanut butter. He had to make a second trip back to the kitchen to fill his pink cup with fresh-squeezed orange juice.

After breakfast, Henry and Benny helped Mrs. McGregor clean up. "There's not even a crumb left on your plate to scrape into the garbage, Benny!" Henry said. "Here's a dishtowel so you can dry these plates. I'm going to see how Jessie and Violet are doing on the cat carrier they're making in the garage. We want to bring the cat along when we help Jessie with her paper route. Maybe someone along the way will know who her owner is."

Benny was having a great time teasing Patches with a thread hanging from the dishtowel. "I wish she could belong to us," he said.

"She belongs to us for now, at least until we find her owner," Henry said. "I'm going out to the garage. See you in a few minutes."

Thanks to fourteen-year-old Henry's part-time summer job at Seed's Hardware Store, the Aldens now had a well-equipped workshop in their grandfather's garage. Henry had stacked up scrap lumber, jars of shiny nails and tacks, and the excellent tools Mr. Seed had lent him. The Aldens loved to fix things that were broken and build whatever they needed.

Today they needed a cat carrier, and Jessie was busy making one when Henry came into the garage. "The extra screening you brought back from the hardware store fits just right over this wooden fruit-box carrier, Henry," Jessie told her brother.

"Good job, Jessie," Henry said when he saw the cat carrier. "Now, what're you up to, Violet?"

Violet was bent over some drawings at the end of the workbench. She held up a handful of FOUND CAT posters she had made. "Do you think anyone will recognize Patches?" she asked.

"I don't think there's another cat in Greenfield with a triangle on her nose like this one," Henry answered.

Benny, too, had something to add when he came out to the garage. "Here's my blanket," he said. He folded the blanket so it fit into the carrier. "She's all set."

Henry looked around the garage, then out in the backyard. "Now all we need is the cat," he said.

That was the hard part. Patches had just

discovered Grandfather Alden's vegetable garden. She was running in and out of the poles he had set up to grow his pea vines.

Jessie went into the house and came out again. "Here's a spoonful of Mrs. Mc-Gregor's tuna fish. Maybe Patches will come over to eat it, and we can catch her that way."

Benny laughed. "No one can turn down Mrs. McGregor's good tuna fish, especially a cat."

When Patches smelled the fish, she ran to Jessie. She quickly licked the spoon, then cleaned her face and paws carefully. This gave Jessie a chance to get the cat into the carrier.

"It's a great box, Jessie, but I don't think she much likes it," Henry told his sister.

Patches wasn't just meowing now. She was howling mad.

In between the howls, the Aldens heard the thud of Jessie's newspapers hitting the curb. "My papers are here," Jessie said. "Let's fold them up quickly so we have plenty of time to talk to people along the way."

When all the papers were folded, everyone set out to deliver them just the way Jessie did. Even Benny was careful to place each newspaper on the porch mat and not just toss it across the yard.

"No one's up this early on our street," Henry said when he came back for another armload of papers. "I'll do the next street. Maybe more people will be out. I'll ask them about the cat."

But there was no one to ask. People in Greenfield were still asleep. The Aldens didn't see anyone until they reached Acorn Street.

"There's Mr. Clover delivering milk and eggs," Benny said. "Mr. Clover! Mr. Clover! Do you know this cat?"

Mr. Clover put down his milk crate and looked into the cat carrier. Patches sniffed at Mr. Clover's hand.

"I sure do," Mr. Clover said. "Belongs to one of my customers, Miss Newcombe, over on Fox Den Road. How did you folks happen to get her?"

The Aldens all talked at once.

"Whoa." Mr. Clover smiled. "How about you, Benny? You're always full of good stories."

Benny took a deep breath and told Mr. Clover all about how Patches had showed up thumping at the window the night before.

Everyone expected Mr. Clover to smile when Benny got to the part about reading the note all by himself. But Mr. Clover wasn't smiling at all.

"You say the note wasn't signed?" He looked upset. "That's pretty odd, I must say. Up until I ran into you, I thought Miss Newcombe had gone on a trip and forgotten to cancel her weekly order for milk and eggs. Went there today, and the gate was locked up tight. Got a box of stuff to bring back to the dairy," he said. He pointed into his truck.

"Why don't you head over to Miss Newcombe's while I finish my route? She lives at 264 Fox Den Road. Maybe she's there by now. Tell her I'll make another run by at the end of my route if she'll just give me a call. I like to check on my older customers when I don't see them around. Miss Newcombe is old and has no family left, so I keep an eye on her when I can. She's very private, though, so I try not to meddle."

After Mr. Clover's bright blue truck pulled away, the Aldens finished the rest of the route quickly. Even Jessie tossed the last few papers up to the porches instead of delivering them by hand. Everyone wanted to get to Fox Den Road as soon as they could.

"What Mr. Clover said doesn't make sense," Henry said when he delivered the last of the newspapers. "Miss Newcombe might have left town too quickly to cancel her order with Mr. Clover. But why did she take the time to write a note and deliver her cat to our house?"

Jessie was puzzled. "And why didn't she sign the note?"

"Oh, where, oh, where is your owner, little cat?" Violet asked.

Patches whined in answer to Violet's question.

CHAPTER 3

No Trespassing!

Fox Den Road was narrow and twisted. Benny didn't take any chances with his wagon or Patches as the Aldens walked along. He kept his red wagon as far to the side as he could so that cars could get by.

Screech! Screech! Everyone heard the noise when they neared the mailbox marked 264. Benny nearly tipped over the wagon at the awful sound.

"What was that sound, Henry?" Violet asked.

Jessie and Henry had run ahead. "It was

these iron gates closing!" Jessie yelled back
to Violet and Benny. "Someone just
slammed them shut on us!"

The Aldens walked up to the rusted iron
gate that blocked the driveway. Next to the
gate was a freshly painted sign in dripping
black letters: No Trespassing! This Means
You!

"Does that mean me, too?" Benny asked
Jessie. People usually wanted to meet Benny
Alden, not chase him away.

"It means everybody," Henry said.

Violet tried to calm the cat. "They can't
mean Patches. This is her home!"

Jessie was careful not to get wet paint on
her clothes. "This sign is brand-new," she
said. "Someone is in there, but we didn't see
who it was." Jessie was twelve and not a bit
put off by the sign. She tried to shake open
the gate.

"It's no use, Jessie," Violet told her sister.
"That padlock is locked tight."

The Aldens stared at the house from outside the gate. Tall, dark evergreens covered
most of the house. Unlike the other homes

they had passed, there were no cheery lights on, or people making breakfast in their kitchens. The windows above the tall front door looked like big blank eyes. The drapes in every window on the first floor were pulled shut.

"Watch out! Watch out!" Henry and Jessie yelled when a rusty pickup truck roared up Fox Den Road out of nowhere. Violet felt gravel hit her legs. Benny nearly tipped over the wagon again.

"It's turning around. Step back!" Henry warned. He pushed his brother and sisters even farther back from the road.

The truck made a sharp turn in the middle of the narrow road and roared back past the children. Again, pieces of gravel peppered everyone's legs.

Henry was angry but not afraid. He chased the truck halfway down Fox Den Road. He wanted to catch it and yell at the driver. The truck sped around the corner and left Henry behind, shaking his fist.

He was still angry when he got back to his brother and sisters. "I bet the men in that

truck didn't want anyone to see them going into Miss Newcombe's property," he said. "That must be why they turned around when they saw us. I couldn't read the sign on the side. All I could make out was 'Wolf D-E-M,' or something like that."

The Aldens tried to calm themselves down. Jessie pulled burrs from the cuffs of Benny's pants. Her hands were shaking. "Are you all right, Benny?"

"I'm not scared," he said in a small voice.

Violet brushed her scratched legs. "That truck nearly ran us over!" she said.

Henry put his arm around Violet. "Well, they won't do it again," he said in a strong voice. "I want to come back here later and get to the bottom of this!"

Violet and Benny still looked pale and frightened and not at all eager to come back to this place again. Jessie took several deep gulps of air and tried to look brave. But her hands were still shaking, and her legs felt rubbery.

When everyone felt a little safer they set off for the animal shelter again. No speeding

trucks passed the Aldens this time. Still, all
of them turned around every few minutes to
make sure they wouldn't be surprised again.
That truck had come *so* close. Everyone
stayed to the far edge of the road, just in
case.

The sight of the Greenfield Animal Shelter
made them all feel a little better. It was in a
big red barn, not too far from Seed's Hardware Store and the Greenfield Bank.

"I like going to work in a barn that's practically in the middle of our town," Benny
said to his brother and sisters. "Especially a
red one."

"Me, too," Jessie said. She put her arm
around Benny to give him a squeeze. She
was glad that he was feeling better after their
upsetting morning.

"See you at lunchtime when I get off from
work," Henry told Jessie, Violet, and Benny
when they reached the small parking lot at
the shelter. "Tell Dr. Scott that Mr. Seed is
giving me some leftover shingles from the
store. I'll use them to fix up that rundown
toolshed in back of the shelter. It will make

a good kennel once we clean it out and patch it up."

After Henry left, Benny lifted Patches from her carrier.

"Uh-oh," Jessie warned Benny. "You'd better put her back inside. That dog is coming straight for her."

Sure enough, a black and white dog with one floppy ear was headed straight for Patches. Behind him was a little boy trying hard to hang onto a leash.

"I'm sorry," said a woman with the little boy when she came over to the Aldens. "This dog is very nervous around all these animals."

Benny was still holding Patches. For some reason, she didn't seem one bit scared of the large dog. The dog sniffed at the cat, then rubbed his nose against Patches's nose.

"Mom, look. Fred is kissing this cat," the little boy said. "If we can't keep Fred, can we get a cat like this one, Mom?"

The woman bent down to talk with her little boy. She spoke softly, but the Aldens heard every word. "Maybe we can think about that, Jeffrey. I wish we could keep Fred, but we'll lose our apartment if we bring him home again. It's too bad the shelter can't take him today. I just don't know what we're going to do with him."

Jessie coughed. "I'm Jessie Alden, and this is my brother, Benny, and my sister, Violet. We're volunteers at the shelter this summer. I'm sure the shelter will take in your dog. They accept every animal."

The woman shook Jessie's outstretched hand. "I'm Susan O'Connor, and this is my little boy, Jeffrey. I wish what you said were true," Mrs. O'Connor told Jessie. "But the people in the shelter said they're closing down in two weeks, and as of today they can't take any more animals."

"That can't be true!" Violet said in alarm.

"I'm afraid it is," Mrs. O'Connor said. "I explained that Fred isn't even our dog, and that we found him wandering around last night in a parking lot. But we were told they don't even know what they're going to do with the animals they already have."

Now Jessie's voice was full of worry.

"There must be a misunderstanding. The shelter would never close down."

Mrs. O'Connor sighed. "I wish that were true, but the people inside seemed very certain. I even explained how I had already tried to find Fred's owner this morning. See, there's part of an address on his tag."

Jessie took a look at the tag. "It says, '264 Fox,' then the rest is worn off. Why, we were just at 264 Fox Den Road ourselves," Jessie told Mrs. O'Connor. "This calico cat lives there, too."

"We went to the house where this cat came from," Violet explained, "but no one was home."

The woman looked upset. "Well, there was someone in the house when we were there. A horrible man."

"With a mean face," the little boy added. "He yelled at us to go away."

Violet petted the friendly dog. "We thought someone named Miss Newcombe lived there. That's her address. But the house was dark."

"And someone put up a mean sign," Benny

added. " 'No Trespassing!' Then a rusty truck almost ran us over."

Jeffrey shivered. "An old bad rusty truck," he said.

His mother explained how a truck had almost run them over that morning, too. As they had stood in the driveway to check the address on the mailbox, the truck came out of the driveway.

"I can't help thinking it must be some other road that starts with the word 'Fox,' " the woman went on. "This nice dog and that sweet cat couldn't possibly belong to such a mean-looking person as the man who chased us away."

The woman sighed. "I must get to work soon. I was going to check if there's another road in Greenfield that starts with 'Fox,' to see if Fred belongs to someone else."

"I deliver newspapers around town and I know most of the roads. I've never seen another road that starts with 'Fox,' " Jessie said. "Maybe you could leave the dog with us. We'll talk to Dr. Scott for you. I'm sure she would take Fred in."

"Look, Mom, Fred likes this girl," Jeffrey said to his mother. "Maybe she can be his mom."

Violet smiled at the little boy. "I'll make sure this dog gets a good home and that you can come and visit," she told the O'Connors. "For now, we'll take him inside and see what Dr. Scott says."

After the O'Connors gave the Aldens their telephone number, Violet walked the dog inside the animal shelter. Behind her, Benny and Jessie carefully carried Patches in her carrier.

The waiting room of the shelter was crowded with barking dogs and meowing cats. One person even had a crow with a broken wing flapping inside a cardboard box.

"What's going on, I wonder?" Jessie said. "I've never seen so many animals here in one day. I'm glad today's our day to work. Dr. Scott's going to need a lot of help."

"I certainly will," the Aldens heard next. Jessie and Violet stepped into the examining room. Benny stayed in the waiting room with Patches and Fred. Dr. Scott, an attractive black woman, was giving a cat a flea bath, which the cat didn't much like. Dr. Scott's own dog, a black poodle named Major, sat right by the doctor's feet. "You children came just in time to help out."

"Dr. Scott, is it true the shelter can't take any more pets?" Violet asked. She handed the animal doctor a fat fluffy towel to dry the wet skinny cat.

Dr. Scott frowned. She looked very upset. "A terrible thing has happened," she began. "Last night we received a telegram from our founder, saying we must close down the shelter in two weeks. We can't use this building or the land around it anymore."

"The Greenfield Animal Shelter can't close down!" Violet cried.

"Can't you ask the founder why they have to shut down the shelter?" Jessie wanted to know.

Dr. Scott stopped rubbing the wet cat for a second. "As I've told you, girls, the identity of the shelter's founder has been a secret for many years. We don't know who the person is except that it's someone who must love animals very much."

"Then why would they close the shelter?" Violet asked.

Dr. Scott drained the sink, then ran more warm water into the basin for another flea bath. "I don't know, Violet. I'm very worried. Whoever this person is must be in some trouble to close this shelter after so many years. I've made quite a few phone calls to see if I can solve the mystery of our founder's identity."

At the sound of the word *mystery*, Benny stuck his head into the examining room. "We solved a mystery today, Dr. Scott, and now we need another one!"

"Do you now, Benny?" Dr. Scott answered. "And what mystery did you solve so early in the day?"

Benny picked up the cat carrier and showed Patches to Dr. Scott. "A cat and dog mystery," he said. He called Fred over. "We think these animals belong to a lady named Miss Newcombe, and she lives on Fox Den

Road. Except somebody mean is there, and we almost got run over. But we're going to go back again. Henry said so."

"You're a good detective, Benny," Dr. Scott told her youngest helper. "These animals do belong to Clara Newcombe. That's her dog, Lad, and her cat, Patches. She brings them for checkups along with many of her other pets. I wonder how these two got loose."

"Patches didn't get loose," Jessie said. "Someone dropped her off at our house with a note saying she needed a good home. A little boy and his mother found Fred, I mean Lad, wandering around in a parking lot."

Dr. Scott looked alarmed. "Oh, my. I'll have to look into this. Miss Newcombe would never give her animals away or let them wander off."

" 'Morning, Dr. Scott," a white-haired man carrying a black-haired cat said as he came into the examining room. "Wondered if you heard anything from Clara lately. She or somebody dropped off Midnight here in my barn last night. The Newcombe place is locked tight. Not like Clara to go off without making arrangements for her pets."

"It certainly isn't, Jeb," the animal doctor told the man. "Something very strange seems to be going on with Clara Newcombe. If I weren't up to my eyebrows in animals, I'd look into it right away. But my first job is to see what I can do about all these strays. Why, I haven't even a matchbox to keep a mouse in!"

The Aldens looked at each other without saying a word. Then Jessie made an announcement. "We have something bigger than a matchbox, Dr. Scott. Much bigger. Something that could shelter a lot of your animals."

"And what would that be?" the doctor asked.

"Our boxcar!" Jessie, Violet, and Benny cried out at the same time.

Dr. Scott looked surprised. "You mean the boxcar you lived in before your grandfather found you?"

Jessie's big brown eyes were shining. "Yes. Grandfather had it moved to our backyard.

We use it as a playhouse, but it would make a good kennel for some of your strays. Henry's been helping Mr. Seed put up new fences this summer. He gets to keep the old fences and chicken wire. We could use them to build animal cages inside the boxcar."

Violet looked up at Dr. Scott's thoughtful face. "You've taught us so much about taking care of animals, Dr. Scott. I know we could do a good job taking care of your strays until we find homes for them."

"I'll walk them and feed them every day," Benny said. "I gave this cat the rest of my blueberries and ice cream last night. These animals would be happy in our boxcar. So would that crow out there."

Dr. Scott smoothed back Benny's hair. "You know, Benny, I think even that crow would like your boxcar. But one thing."

Benny looked up at Dr. Scott. "What's that?"

"Just give the crow plain blueberries. No ice cream."

Benny nodded. "Okay, no ice cream. Just blueberries."

CHAPTER 4

The Hidden Notebooks

That day when the Greenfield Library bell rang out at noon, the Aldens could hardly pull themselves away from their work at the shelter. Jessie wanted to finish lining the indoor cages with newspapers. Violet was busy making flyers for adopting cats and dogs and more FOUND CAT notices to put up around town. And, for a change, Benny Alden wasn't chattering or hungry.

"Even animal doctors stop for lunch," Dr. Scott said when she found the three Aldens still hard at work at twelve-fifteen.

Dr. Scott smiled down at Benny. "I've never known you to forget about your lunch."

Everyone was laughing when Dr. Scott put up the CLOSED FOR LUNCH sign on the front door of the shelter. "Have a nice big lunch so you can tackle that old shed when you get back with Henry. Maybe by then I'll have some information about our mystery founder. I'm going to spend my lunchtime making phone calls. Now off you go."

On the short walk to the hardware store, Violet stopped to post one of her FOUND CAT signs on a telephone pole in front of the bank. "Our phone number is on these posters. I hope Grandfather or Mrs. McGregor is home in case anyone calls," she said.

Benny ran up ahead. He expected to see Henry waiting in front of Seed's Hardware the way he usually did at lunchtime every day. But Henry was nowhere around.

"Maybe we came too late," Jessie said. She tried the door and it opened. "That's strange. Usually Mr. Seed closes up right at noon. He must have a customer."

In fact, Mr. Seed had three customers.

One man was at the cash register where Henry was carefully counting out money. The Aldens could see two other men in back with Mr. Seed.

"Don't bother with the change, sonny," the man told Henry. "It's not worth counting just a lot of loose coins."

That didn't stop Henry. "My grandfather says every dollar starts with a penny, sir. Besides, Mr. Seed wouldn't like it if his customers didn't get the change they were due."

"Whatever you say, sonny, but make it fast." The man grabbed the change Henry gave him and shoved it into his pocket without even counting it.

Everyone looked up when Mr. Seed came in from the loading dock with the two men following behind. Mr. Seed was talking slowly, but the men didn't seem to be paying any attention.

"Now, you'll want to drive slowly and avoid any bumps with that box of dynamite in your trunk," Mr. Seed said. "Your whole car could blow up if you hit a pothole too hard, you know."

"No problem, old man," one of the men said to Mr. Seed.

Mr. Seed noticed Jessie, Violet, and Benny waiting for Henry, who was busy looking for a receipt book. "Henry, why don't you leave those receipts so you can have lunch with your brother and sisters? I'll get them signed."

One of the men stepped up to the register where Mr. Seed was filling out the receipt book. "No need to sign anything, is there, mister? This is a cash deal. No need for receipts. We're going to use that dynamite. Don't worry, we won't be back to exchange it for one of these flowerpots or maybe a nice pack of marigold seeds."

The man and his two friends seemed to find this very funny and laughed loudly. The Aldens could see Mr. Seed's face turn red. He was proud of everything in his store, including the flowerpots.

Jessie couldn't bear to see Mr. Seed upset. "Excuse me, Mr. Seed. I'd like two starter pots for geraniums," she said.

"Sure thing, Jessie," Mr. Seed said in a

shaky voice. "And what about you, Violet? Can I get you anything?"

"Just a piece of tape to put up this FOUND CAT sign. We found Miss Newcombe's animals, but we can't find her. Maybe one of your customers will see my sign and tell us where she is."

At this, all three men stared hard at the Aldens. The man who had made fun of the flowerpots stepped up to Jessie. "You kids didn't happen to follow us here, now, did you?"

"Of course not," Jessie answered. "We came to meet our brother for lunch. And buy some flower seeds for our grandfather's garden. May I have two packs of the marigolds, Mr. Seed?"

Mr. Seed didn't answer right away. He was studying the way the three men were staring at the Aldens. He didn't like what he saw one bit.

"Of course, of course, Jessie," he finally answered. "But let's let these customers out first." He hurried the men to the front door. "Good day," he told them, though it was plain from his voice that this hadn't been a good day at all. The brass bell at the top of the door jingled when he opened the door, then jingled again when he shut it and turned the big brass lock so the men couldn't come back in.

Everyone started talking at once. "Who were those men, Mr. Seed?" Jessie asked first. "And why did they talk to you and Henry that way?"

Mr. Seed wiped his forehead with a handkerchief. The Aldens could see he wasn't his usual cheery self. His hands shook, and his eyes darkened. "I got a call a few days ago from one of them, I'm not sure which one. They're all demanding and impatient. Said they were from a construction company and then ordered a box of dynamite, which I had to get special from one of my suppliers. When they came to pick it up, I almost changed my mind about selling it to them, but they had a purchase order from a construction company upstate."

"Have you or Henry ever seen them before?" Jessie asked.

Henry frowned and seemed to be thinking hard. "That's the odd thing. I kept thinking I'd seen them somewhere, but I can't figure out where or when."

Mr. Seed locked up the register. "I don't even like to take money from people like that. And I didn't like the once-over they gave all of you when you came into the store. That's why I wanted them to leave before the four of you went outside."

"They did look at us kind of funny," Benny said. "But not really *funny*. That one guy looked mean when Violet said she wanted to put up the flyer to find Miss Newcombe."

Violet hugged the sheets of paper close to her. "Why would that bother them, I wonder? Well, I don't care. I am just going to post these all over town. We have Miss Newcombe's pets, and now we need to find Miss Newcombe."

"Well, here's some tape, Violet," Mr. Seed said. "When you go back to the animal shelter later, you can tape up a few of your flyers on the outside of my windows. For now, I think it would be a good idea to eat your lunch in here, so that those men are well out of town when you go back to the shelter. Henry and I loaded up the truck already with plenty of shingles and nails and whatever else you need to fix that toolshed Dr. Scott wants repaired."

"Would you like a meat loaf sandwich, Mr. Seed?" Jessie asked when she opened her knapsack. "I'm not too hungry today. You can have mine."

Mr. Seed shook his head. "I'm afraid those men took my appetite with them. They're up to no good, and I'm sorry I ever let them in the store. No, I'm not hungry, either. But you should eat. You'll need all the energy you can muster when you work on that old toolshed. Last time I was at the shelter, I noticed there was a lot of water damage on one side. Just taking out the rotted shingles is going to be a big job."

"We like big jobs," Benny announced, "so I'd better eat two sandwiches for lunch!"

This made everyone laugh and realize they were hungry after all. Jessie unwrapped all the sandwiches and put a fat pickle next to each one. "There's plenty of ice-cold lemonade, too," she said as she twisted the cap off a tall red thermos.

When the library bell rang a half hour later, the Aldens packed all their lunch things in Mr. Seed's truck along with the materials he was giving to the shelter. Mr. Seed drove on a dirt path in back of the red barn that led to the far end of the property.

"I hope you won't be doing all this hard work for nothing," Mr. Seed told the Aldens when he stopped the truck in front of the old toolshed. "I've heard the shelter's closing in a couple of weeks, so Dr. Scott may not need the extra space."

Jessie looked at Mr. Seed. "The animals need more space now, and I just know we can help Dr. Scott track down the founder of the shelter before the deadline. We have to — we just have to."

"Of course," Mr. Seed said gently. "Now you folks give me a call when you need some other supplies from my store. I've got plenty of chicken wire, wood boards — lots of things I know you could use in that boxcar you all told me about. All you have to do is ask, okay?"

"Okay!" the Aldens all said at once.

Soon everyone was busy pulling out rotted boards and lining up the new shingles to replace the old ones.

After a few minutes, Violet spoke up. "I wonder if Dr. Scott was able to find out anything while we were gone."

"I found two pups for your boxcar," everyone heard next as Dr. Scott came out to see how the Aldens were doing. In each arm the animal doctor was carrying a German shepherd puppy they hadn't seen before. "These pups will be big dogs in no time, and the cages we have here will be much too small for them."

Benny held one of the squirming dogs in his arms while Jessie held the other. "Did you have any luck finding out about the founder of the shelter, Dr. Scott?" Jessie asked.

Dr. Scott shook her head. "I'm afraid not, Jessie. After you left, I still had so many shots to give and so many other calls to make about getting homes for these strays, I didn't get a chance to make any other calls. Then there's Miss Newcombe to check on, too. Everything always happens at the same time. But you've all been a big help tending to all these strays. And Henry here has been sent from heaven."

"We'll have this old shed fixed up by this afternoon since Mr. Seed gave me the rest of the day off," Henry told Dr. Scott. "Then you won't have to double up so many animals."

"That'll be a great relief," Dr. Scott said. "These poor animals can start living like dogs and cats and not like sardines." She peeked into the dusty old shed. "I'll call for the junk man to remove that old desk and those chairs in there to make more space."

"Oh, no, we want them!" Jessie cried out.

Dr. Scott winked at everyone. "I was teasing! After watching the four of you save every bit of string, every scrap of paper, and every bottle and can this summer, I knew you would find some use for these old pieces of furniture. I'll arrange to have everything sent to your grandfather's, so don't you worry."

"We'll use the desk and chairs for an office in our garage," Jessie told the doctor. "We want our shelter to be just like the Greenfield Animal Shelter."

"Judging by the excellent repair job you're doing on this old shed, I know you'll turn your boxcar into a safe place for my strays," Dr. Scott said before heading back to the barn.

"I like tearing down old things, so I can fix them up again," Jessie said when she held up a new shingle for Henry to nail in.

"So do I," Benny said. He easily pulled off the last few boards from the rotted section of wall. "Hey, look at this!" he called out a few minutes later. "There's something stuck between these last two boards."

"Looks like some old black notebooks," Henry said when he took a close look at what Benny had discovered. "On the cover it says, 'Property of Jacob Kisco.' "

Jessie, who loved old books, took a closer

look. "Jacob Kisco must have been a dairy farmer. Look, this page tells how much milk his cows gave and how much food they ate."

Benny was disappointed. "Just a bunch of old notes about cows. Nothing good."

"Why, Benny, we can use these to keep track of *our* animals when we set up our shelter," Jessie said.

"You and Violet can do that," Benny said. "I want to feed the animals and play with them."

Henry, Jessie, and Violet couldn't help laughing. Benny always liked jobs where he could run and play and not have to stay still for too long.

"Let's finish up here," Jessie said. "There'll be time to look through these old notebooks when we get home."

Henry put the heavy books in the top drawer of the old desk. He shut the drawer and went back to work measuring and hammering.

CHAPTER 5

Boxcar Days

The Aldens spent all their time getting the boxcar ready for business. Jessie and Violet made good use of the leftover boards Henry brought back from Seed's Hardware Store. In no time, they had added four new shelves to the boxcar to store the food, dishes, blankets, and old towels they needed to feed their orphaned animals and keep them warm. On opening day, the needy orphans included four cats, three fat white rabbits, one crow, and three dogs.

Benny's job was to sort and clean the

dishes they had used in the old boxcar days. "There are just enough dishes so that each animal gets one water dish and one food dish," he told Violet and Jessie.

Out back, Henry finished framing the last few yards of chicken wire with old fence posts. "Come on, Lad. Here you go, fellas," he said when he led all the dogs into the spacious dog run.

When everything was ready, Benny ran inside and brought out Mr. Alden to take a look at what they had all built.

"Well, Grandfather, what do you think of our shelter?" Jessie asked Mr. Alden.

Mr. Alden took a step up the tree stump that led into the boxcar. "Why, this looks more like a fine hotel than a shelter for strays," Mr. Alden told Jessie when he looked around.

"This side is just for cats," Jessie explained. She pointed to the roomy chicken-wire cages on one side of the boxcar.

Benny pointed to the shelves Violet and Jessie had put up. "That's where we keep the old dishes we had in the boxcar," Benny announced. "I have to fill each one with water and food twice a day and put them out for each animal. That black cat only likes dry food, and Patches only likes tuna fish."

"Look at what we built out here, Grandfather," Violet said when everyone came outside again.

"What a fine dog run," Mr. Alden said. "Lad and those pups have plenty of room to chase each other, don't they? They certainly don't look like the sad orphans Dr. Scott dropped off last night. They're right at home. Good job."

"Thank you, Grandfather," Henry said.

"I guess I'll go back inside and see what I can do for Watch," Mr. Alden said. "Listen to that sad whining. He really doesn't like the *whole* family out here with all these new animals."

After Mr. Alden left, Jessie checked her clipboard of things to do. "Now that the animals are all settled, we need to fix up an office in the garage. There are cases of pet food to order, prescriptions to get filled, and notes to take for Dr. Scott. She'll want to know everything when she comes by this afternoon."

Benny Alden wasn't too interested in office work. Not when there were so many animals to play with. "Can I stay outside and play with the puppies, Henry?"

Henry was already up on a ladder in Mr. Alden's garage and putting in long shelves for bandages, animal-care books, and the curious black notebooks no one had had time to look at again. "Go ahead, Benny," Henry called down from the ladder. "What good's having an animal shelter in your own backyard if you can't run around like a puppy?"

When Benny came back an hour later, the garage looked almost like Dr. Scott's office at the Greenfield Animal Shelter. Henry and Violet finished putting away the medical supplies, while Jessie wrote careful reports on each of the animals in their care.

"I think I might use these old farmer's notebooks to keep everything organized," Jessie told Henry and Violet. "One of them could be for ordering food, another for our reports to Dr. Scott, and the third one for anything else we need to write down."

Violet began reading over the wrinkled, torn pages of one of the notebooks. "I'm glad we're only taking care of pet animals, not real farm animals," she said. "Mr. Kisco's cows needed forty-seven bales of hay over one long winter."

"It's hard to believe there was so much farmland right here in Greenfield," Jessie said. "There aren't many farms nearby nowadays."

Henry looked over Violet's shoulder. "Mr. Seed said the farms started two roads over from Main Street back then, from Fox Den Road all the way to Burrville," Henry said. "Now, of course, all the land near town is worth too much to keep as farmland. That must be why someone wants the animal shelter."

"Hey, Jessie, something just fell out," Benny said when he came into the garage. He bent down to pick up a long yellow envelope that had fallen out of the notebook Jessie was holding. "It says 'D-E-E-D' on the envelope. Is that like what Grandfather says people should do — a good deed?"

"This is another kind of deed, Benny," Jessie said. She carefully unfolded the thick sheet of paper. "This is a legal paper that says who owns certain land. There's an old map attached. See?"

"Let me see it, too, Jessie," Henry said to his sister. "Maybe it's something important that belongs to the Greenfield Animal Shelter."

Henry studied the old document. "Jacob Kisco deeds fifty acres of land to Silas Newcombe," he read. Henry shook his head. "Didn't Grandfather say that when he was a little boy, Miss Newcombe's father, Silas, gave the schools free milk and ice cream that came from his farm?"

Jessie looked thoughtful. "That's right. But if the deed has her father's name on it, why was it hidden away in this old book in that broken-down toolshed? Why shouldn't Miss Newcombe have it in a safe place?"

Violet had a worried look on her face. "I just know something must be wrong with Miss Newcombe. I have a feeling."

"Dr. Scott will be here soon to check on the animals," Jessie said. "Maybe she can figure out what this deed is all about."

The Aldens were still talking about Miss Newcombe when they heard Dr. Scott's station wagon pull into their grandfather's driveway.

But there was no time to tell Dr. Scott anything. She arrived, out of breath and in a hurry. She apologized to everyone. "I'm sorry to be in such a rush, but trying to clear out the shelter in such a short time has cut into my medical work."

The Aldens could see this was no time to bring up the land deed. Dr. Scott was already out back with her medical bag. As she visited the animals one by one, the children reported on each of them.

Henry let Dr. Scott into the dog run where Lad and the two puppies were sound asleep in a heap on top of each other. "The two pups started regular food this morning," Jessie told the doctor. "They didn't whine at all during the night."

"Maybe they just needed more food," Dr.

Scott said. "And having this safe new home helps them sleep through the night, too."

Benny took hold of Dr. Scott's hand. "Come see the crow," he told her when they stopped in front of the tall, airy birdcage. The crow was sitting on a tree branch Benny had put in the cage. "This crow ate two handfuls of blueberries from Grandfather's blueberry bushes last night, but no ice cream."

"I see he trusts you, Benny," Dr. Scott said. She reached into the cage and wrapped both her hands around the bird to check his wing. "He's well fed, now, and this wing is mending beautifully. In another few days, leave the cage door open. He may be able to make a short flight to those blueberry bushes himself and come back to the safety of this cage until his wing is completely healed. Now how are those rabbits doing?"

"They're right here," Benny said. He led Dr. Scott to the rabbit hutch. "I let them out to play, and they ate two heads of Grandfather's lettuce from the garden! I think I should bring them their dinner *inside* the cage from now on."

"I think so, too, or we won't have any salad for the rest of the summer," Henry laughed.

Dr. Scott finished her checkups. "Well, I see these animals don't need me! Is there anything else we should talk about?"

"Yes, there is something," Jessie answered. "It's not about the animals, though, but it might have something to do with Miss Newcombe."

"Ah, yes, Miss Newcombe." Dr. Scott sighed. "I haven't forgotten her, you know. After many calls, I finally reached the new caretaker who is looking after her house. He says she's away visiting relatives. I've only had one short conversation with this man, but something bothers me. With everything that's going on at the shelter lately, I just haven't had time to figure out what it is."

"Didn't Mr. Clover tell us she didn't have family left?" Henry asked everyone.

Jessie's eyes opened wide. "He did! Then how could Miss Newcombe be visiting relatives?"

Dr. Scott's face lit up. "Of course! That's what was bothering me. I knew Clara Newcombe didn't have any relatives, but I had so much on my mind I forgot all about that." Dr. Scott patted Jessie's shoulder. "Good thinking."

"Maybe you can help with something now," Jessie said. She opened up the farmer's black notebook.

Benny started first. "We found a deed in this old book. A deed is a piece of paper about land."

Dr. Scott took out a pair of reading glasses from the pocket of her white jacket. She read over the old piece of paper Jessie had given her. "Hmm. If I'm not mistaken, this seems to be a deed for the land the Greenfield Shelter is on. One thing puzzles me, though. This deed includes Miss Newcombe's property as well."

Violet took another look at the paper. "Maybe when the deed was written, both pieces of property were part of the same land."

Dr. Scott wiped her glasses with her handkerchief. "You've all discovered a very interesting document here. Of course, this deed is fifty years old, so it may not be legal anymore. The only way to find out is to visit the Land Records Office at the state capital."

Henry took another look at the piece of paper. "I'm going to ask Grandfather about this. His old friend, Elizabeth Thompson, is a lawyer who works at the state capital. Maybe we can take a trip up there and see if there's a record of this deed on file."

"That's an excellent idea, Henry," Dr. Scott said, "so I'll leave the deed with you. Meanwhile, I'll keep up my own investigation here in Greenfield about the shelter property," she said before getting into her station wagon.

As the Aldens waved to the animal doctor, they heard the telephone ringing inside the house.

"Mrs. McGregor and Grandfather said we should answer the phone for the rest of the day. They said every time they answer, someone hangs up," Jessie said as she ran up the porch stairs behind Violet.

Violet got to the phone first. "Maybe it's someone who saw my flyer for the two Ger-

man shepherd puppies," she gasped. "Boxcar Animal Shelter, Violet Alden speaking."

No one spoke at the other end, but Violet could tell someone was there.

"This is the Boxcar Animal — " she began to say before she was cut off by a rough voice.

"You're gonna need a lot more than a boxcar for your animal shelter, little girl," the voice said. "You're gonna need a freight train a mile long for all the animals that'll be leaving the real shelter any day now."

Violet couldn't find her voice to answer back. Jessie took the phone receiver from her hand. "Who is this, and what do you want?"

"Glad you asked, miss," the voice said back. "I want you to stop looking for the old lady and stop asking a lot of nosy questions. That's what I want, you hear?"

Jessie was still holding the phone when the person hung up without another word.

"He hung up," she said quietly.

By this time, Mr. Alden and Mrs. Mc-Gregor had gathered near the phone to find out about the mystery caller.

Mrs. McGregor was very upset when she

saw Jessie's and Violet's frightened faces. She shook her rolling pin at the phone. "You know, that's the third or fourth time someone has called here today. Only whenever your grandfather or I answered, they hung up."

Mr. Alden put his arm around Violet. "What did the caller want? Did the voice sound at all familiar?"

"The man said we'd need a freight train, not a boxcar, for all the animals that will have to leave the shelter soon," Violet told her grandfather.

Jessie picked up the receiver in case the person was still there, but all she heard was the dial tone. "He said to stop looking for Miss Newcombe and to stop asking nosy questions."

"Well, he said the wrong thing to this family," Henry said when he joined the group around the phone. "We're just going to make sure we look even harder for Miss Newcombe and ask even more nosy questions!"

CHAPTER 6

Raining Cats and Dogs

At the sound of howling, Violet sat up in bed. "Lad!" she cried when she recognized his special howl.

She slipped from her bed and went to the window. Outside it was raining softly and too foggy to see very well. For a second, Violet thought she saw a grayish figure move across the lawn. But when she rubbed the fogged window to see better, there was no one there except the three sleeping rabbits and one sleeping crow in their outdoor cages.

"I must have dreamed Lad was howling," she said. She yawned and rubbed her eyes, then went back to bed.

Finally a real animal woke her up for good. "Oh, Watch, it's you," she said and yawned as he pushed against her leg with his nose. "Finally, it's morning," she said with an even bigger yawn. "What a long night. I'm *so* tired."

Violet heard the clink of glasses and silverware coming from the kitchen. Everyone's up already, she told herself. She ran her fingers through her brown hair and quickly pulled on some lavender shorts and a flowered T-shirt.

"Good morning, sleepyhead," Mr. Alden said to his granddaughter when she appeared in the kitchen.

"Are you feeling well, Violet?" Mrs. McGregor asked. "You look a bit peaked this morning."

"I *am* tired, Mrs. McGregor," Violet told the housekeeper. "The rain woke me up during the night. I thought I heard Lad howling."

"Rain? I don't think it rained," Mrs. McGregor said as she broke an egg into the frying pan. "It's bright and sunny, just like yesterday. You'll feel fine once you have a nice big breakfast like Benny's."

"I can't eat right now," Violet said. "Not until I check the boxcar."

The animals heard Violet coming and started up some real howling. Violet slid open the heavy boxcar door and looked inside. She hardly ever raised her voice, but this morning she did. "Henry! Jessie! Benny! Grandfather! Come out back!"

Watch was the first to bound out to see what the excitement was all about. When he reached the boxcar, he didn't like what he saw at all. Another dog! Another cat! Was there no end to the animals who were taking over the Alden house?

"Where did this pooch come from?" Henry asked.

A large white dog with black markings looked out at everyone with frightened eyes.

"And look over here!" Benny said.

"There's a big gray cat in this cage! Where did it come from?"

"Who are these two animals?" Mr. Alden asked his grandchildren. "Do you suppose Dr. Scott dropped them off from the shelter last night?"

Violet shook her head. "These animals couldn't be from the shelter. They weren't there yesterday."

"Dr. Scott wouldn't just leave them here without letting us know," Jessie added. "Maybe someone was here last night, Violet, and you really did hear something going on."

By this time, the boxcar was noisy with barking dogs, crying cats, and five Aldens all talking at once.

It was Henry who noticed the new dog rubbing noses with Lad. "Lad knows this dog, too!" Henry said. "The hook on the dog's tag broke off, but his collar looks just like Lad's."

"Not just the collar — the whole dog looks like Lad!" Jessie said. "Only this dog is white where Lad is black, and black where Lad is white. They both must belong to Miss New-combe."

"I guess I wasn't dreaming after all," Violet said. "Someone brought these animals here during the night. I wonder who?"

The Aldens heard Jessie's newspapers hit the sidewalk. "You'll have plenty to do today," Mr. Alden said. "Papers to deliver, two new pets to look after, and another mystery to figure out."

Henry was in the boxcar getting leashes for Watch, Lad, and the new dog when all the dogs started howling and barking at the same time. Then Watch broke away and raced to the front yard.

"What's the matter with these dogs?" Violet asked.

"I thought I heard a car door slam," Jessie said.

When the Aldens reached the front yard, all was quiet. The bundle of newspapers was where it was every morning. Everything was still except for a very nervous Watch, trailed by Lad and the new dog, who looked plenty nervous, too.

"I wonder what this is all about," Henry said, trying to calm all three dogs.

Violet checked down the street where the dogs were looking. "I'm sure they didn't bark for nothing, especially Watch. He never barks unless something is wrong."

Jessie bent down to sort out her newspapers. Turning pale, she cried, "Here's what's wrong!" She held up a torn, dirty sheet of paper. "Someone must have just stuck this inside my newspaper bundle after it was dropped off."

Henry grabbed the paper and read it out loud: " 'This is your last warning. Mind your business!' "

"So that's what upset the dogs," Jessie said. "Well, whoever wrote this will have to write a longer note next time, because I'm going to go right on minding Miss Newcombe's business until we find her!"

The Aldens never did a faster job of helping Jessie with her newspaper route. They even set the dogs to work carrying papers up to people's porches, and the route was finished in record time.

"All done," Jessie told everyone when all the newspapers were gone. "Now let's get to Miss Newcombe's house right away. I kept one paper out, and I'm going to deliver it there no matter what!"

The Aldens listened carefully for traffic when they reached Fox Den Road. No rusty pickup truck was going to surprise them this time!

When they got to Miss Newcombe's gate, Jessie whispered, "Look, the NO TRESPASS-ING sign is still up, but the gate's open today. Violet, you and Benny wait out here while Henry and I go up to the house and ring the doorbell."

Violet, Benny, and the three dogs stayed out of sight of the house but well away from the road. They looked on as their brother and sister marched straight up to the house and rang the bell.

When the door finally opened, they heard Jessie's clear voice speak out. "Good morning. I'm delivering free copies of the *Greenfield Daily News* this week. Would you like one?"

Through the bushes, Benny and Violet

could see that the man talking to Jessie was one of the same men who had been at Mr. Seed's hardware store! He was staring angrily at their sister. "We don't want any paper in this house," he finally answered. "And if you see the fellow who put this milk in the cooler, tell him not to come back. We don't want any deliveries. Especially from you snoopy kids, you hear?"

This didn't stop Henry. "Maybe someone else in your house would like our paper," he told the unshaven man. "Home delivery saves a lot of car trips to town. Won't you check with the other people in your household?"

For an answer, Henry got a door slammed in his face.

"Did you see anyone else in there?" Violet asked when Jessie and Henry came back to the gate.

"No one," Henry answered. "Just that man. He was one of the men who bought the dynamite at Mr. Seed's."

Jessie's brown eyes grew large and bright. "You know who else he is? The same man I heard on the phone. I'm sure of it. He finishes what he's saying with 'you hear.' As if we couldn't hear a loud voice like that!"

Violet shivered. "Do you really think it's the same person, Jessie? Why would Miss Newcombe let someone like that live in her house?"

Henry looked worried. "Maybe she didn't let them in, Violet. Maybe they scared her away."

"Well, that man didn't scare these dogs away. Look, they want to go back to the house," Benny cried.

Sure enough, Lad and the white dog were pulling hard on their leashes and half dragging Benny up the driveway toward the house again.

"They know this is their home," Violet cried. "Well, I'm just going to march up there and see what happens. Let's see what the man has to say about that!"

This time, four Aldens and three dogs went up to the porch. Violet rang the bell.

The door flew open. "I told you, I don't want what you're selling, you hear?" the man

shouted when he saw a porch full of Aldens and dogs. "Now, git!" he said.

Suddenly, Lad pulled so hard on the leash, it slipped from Benny's hand. He dashed into the house! Before the Aldens had time to think about their manners, they were in the house, too.

With Watch and the new dog, Benny and Henry flew down a hallway.

"Lad! Lad! Come back!" Benny yelled. He chased the dog to the back of the house.

"You kids stay out of this house and keep those hounds out, too," the man shouted. "I say, get out of here!"

Henry hurried back and stood in front of the man. "We won't leave without our brother or the dogs!" he said. Then Henry ran off again to find Lad.

Jessie stood tall, too. "That black dog and this white one live in this house," she told the man.

"No one lives here but me," the man said.

Violet was shaking, but she spoke up all the same. "Where is Miss Newcombe?" she demanded. "This is *her* home."

The man stepped toward Violet. "And what business is that of yours, little girl? None at all, I say. I'm in charge of this property now, and I don't have to explain anything to trespassers!"

By this time, Henry had caught Lad by the leash, and Benny was right behind. "Don't worry, we're leaving. But you can't keep us from looking for Miss Newcombe," Henry said.

Before anyone could stop Benny, he spoke to the man, too. "We have a deed to her house, and my grandfather is going to bring it to the state capital to see who owns this house."

"We'll see about that!" the man warned. "Now get off this property, you hear?"

When everyone was safe at the end of the driveway, Jessie put her arm around Benny. "Are you all right, Benny?"

"I'm good," Benny said, "but that man is bad. And I think there are other people in that house, too. I heard a door bang and some footsteps while I was chasing Lad."

Henry led his brother and sisters out the

gate. "Benny's right. When I ran to the back of the house to follow Benny and Lad, I thought I saw someone disappear into a back room. Another man. They're the same men who bought the dynamite at Mr. Seed's and who nearly ran us over with their truck."

"I can't believe strange people would be in a nice old woman's house," Violet said. "And to act as if Lad didn't live there! Why, anyone could see both dogs knew that house very well."

When the Aldens peeked through some evergreens at the house, Jessie stared longer than anyone else. "Look, Henry. The truck that tried to run us over is parked back there," she whispered.

Henry took a look. "It's the same pickup truck! That man who answered the door isn't alone in there, I'm sure of it. I'm going to sneak around the side of the house and see what that truck says."

Violet and Benny looked on as Jessie and Henry walked through a clump of trees that led toward the house.

With each footstep, Jessie and Henry

seemed to crack a branch or an acorn or scare a bird out of a bush. They were sure the men in the house could hear every snapped twig and crunched leaf.

"I think we can get a good look through those loose stones," Jessie told Henry when they got to the wall that surrounded the property.

"I'll take out this rock from the wall," Henry said.

A chipmunk dashed out from the space where the rock had been, and Jessie and Henry jumped back.

"Whew!" Henry said.

He and Jessie bent down low. They peered through the wall opening. Now the rusty truck was only a few feet away.

Jessie read the peeling sign on the side of the truck. "It says, 'Wolf Demolition.' In smaller letters it says, 'We take down buildings any size.' " Jessie's eyes opened wide with worry. "Do you think they're going to tear down Miss Newcombe's house, Henry?"

Henry shook his head. "I guess that's why

they bought all that dynamite. But maybe Miss Newcombe hired them for that. This is the last piece of farmland so close to town. It's probably more valuable to build on it than to keep it as a rundown farm. Maybe Miss Newcombe needs money, and wants to sell the land to somebody who wants to build on it."

Henry and Jessie ducked when they heard the door squeak open. They took turns peeking through the stones. The unshaven man stood on the side porch smoking a cigarette while he talked to some other men still inside the house.

"We'll just let her in the house to get her things, and that's all," one deep voice said from inside. "If she even comes back. I think we scared her good."

"Maybe. She's got a few days to get back. Then we'll turn this place into dust," another voice said. "Can't believe the old lady's been sitting on this gold mine, and it ain't even hers. Too bad the boss took so long to get that land search done. We'd better make sure those kids don't start snooping around the

Land Records office at the capital before we get there."

"Don't worry about that," the man on the porch said. "They'll never get there in time." He put out his cigarette in the window box and went inside.

Henry and Jessie could no longer hear the three voices, but they'd heard enough. They crept back through the woods to find Violet and Benny.

"Did you find out anything?" Benny asked.

"We found out that truck is from a demolition company that's going to tear down Miss Newcombe's house," Henry said.

"The men in there said this isn't even her house," Jessie added. "At least that's what we think they said. We only heard a little."

"We heard enough to know that Miss Newcombe's home is in danger," Henry said. "We have to find her, and we have to get the deed up to the state capital right away!"

CHAPTER 7

A Good Deed

The next day, everyone was up early so they could get a fast start on their trip to the state capital. Grandfather's friend, Elizabeth Thompson, who did some work with the Land Records Office, had said they could file the deed immediately.

"Now you make sure to give yourself time to have those peanut butter sandwiches at lunchtime," Mrs. McGregor told everyone as they got into Mr. Alden's roomy car. "I know you'll be hungry."

"I know I will be, too," Benny said.

Jessie checked her long list of chores. "The animals are all fed and walked for the day," she told Mrs. McGregor.

"Don't worry about a thing," Mrs. McGregor said.

"We won't," Mr. Alden said when he backed out his car. "We've got a full tank of gas and the excellent lunch you prepared to keep us all from starving."

Jessie held up the all-important black notebook for Mrs. McGregor to see. "And tucked safely in here is Miss Newcombe's deed."

"It's a good deed!" Benny called out the window to Mrs. McGregor.

Mr. Alden and his grandchildren laughed. "It is *indeed*!" he said. Everyone laughed again, and they were on their way.

But not for long.

"Why is the car slowing down, Grandfather?" Henry said when he heard the car sputter. In a few minutes it stopped dead in the middle of the highway.

Mr. Alden quickly tried to restart the engine, but nothing happened. "I don't know what the problem is, but we have to get out

quickly while the road is clear." Mr. Alden raced to help his grandchildren out of the car.

When everyone was safe, Mr. Alden checked the highway. "Henry, you give a push while I steer the car off the road. No one is coming right now."

But Mr. Alden was wrong. Just when Henry was giving the last strong push to roll the car to the side, Jessie screamed, "Grandfather! Henry! Watch out!"

Henry turned around just in time to see the Wolf Demolition truck whiz by, only inches away from the car.

The Aldens recognized one of the passengers right away. "Looks like you'll be here all day," the unshaven man from Miss Newcombe's house snickered before the truck disappeared in a cloud of oily blue smoke.

"I bet they're going to the state capital," Violet cried.

"Never mind, Violet," Henry said while he and Jessie continued pushing the car. "We have the deed. Even though Miss Thompson said the Land Records Office closes early on

Fridays during the summertime, we still have time to get there before noon."

After the car was safely off the road, Mr. Alden took off his jacket and rolled up his shirtsleeves. "I'm going to check the engine. Maybe we've overheated, or the oil level dropped for some reason. Can't figure out why, though. Jack Vetrano checked out everything just yesterday."

For the next half hour, the Aldens did everything they could think of to get the car started. Nothing worked.

"The water and oil levels seem fine," Mr. Alden said after checking the dipstick. "If I hadn't just filled the gas tank yesterday, I'd almost think we were out of gas."

Henry took out his baseball cap from the backseat and put it on. "Grandfather, I'm going to look for help. Maybe there's a gas station up ahead, and I can get a mechanic back here to take a look at what's wrong."

Henry didn't waste any time jogging off for help. After he disappeared down the road, a few cars stopped by to offer help, but Mr. Alden waved them away, saying his grandson would be bringing back some help very soon.

"There's a red tow truck slowing down!" Benny said awhile later.

The driver jumped down from the truck, and Henry got out on the passenger side. "This is Mr. Hall, Grandfather. He knows everything about cars like yours."

"I'll work fast," Mr. Hall said. "Your grandson, here, told me all about how you have to get to the capital by noon."

Mr. Hall went over and under the car with his tools. From under the car, everyone heard him say, "Maybe you're out of gas."

"It's not likely," Mr. Alden said. "I just had it filled up yesterday, and I didn't drive it until today."

The mechanic took a gas can with a long spout and began pouring gas into the tank.

"Well, let's see if a little gas can get it going. It might push out some air that could be in the gas line," Mr. Hall said as he poured. And poured. "I don't like to say this, sir, but your gas tank seems to be bone dry."

"That's impossible," Henry said. "If my

grandfather said he filled the tank, he filled it."

"Maybe he did, but it's still dry. With gas prices the way they are these days, maybe somebody drained your gas out."

"I have to say I'm quite embarrassed at all this, but you fixed the problem, so give me the bill," Mr. Alden said to the mechanic.

Everyone got into the car, which was soon humming down the highway again.

"I can't figure it, I just can't figure it," Mr. Alden repeated. "I filled this tank with gas when I picked it up from Jack last night."

"I think I know what happened, Grandfather," Henry said. "I think they drained all our gas on purpose because they didn't want us to make this trip to check on the deed. Then they tampered with the gas gauge so you wouldn't know anything was wrong."

"You're probably right, Henry," Mr. Alden agreed. "In any case, we have the deed, and they don't."

When the Aldens met Miss Thompson in the capitol lobby at twenty to twelve, she didn't know a thing about the three men. "I'm sorry, James," she said to Mr. Alden. "There've been hundreds of people going through the lobby all morning. I can't say I noticed three suspicious men in all these crowds. But that does give us even more reason to hurry! It's nearly closing time."

Everyone raced behind Miss Thompson up three flights of marble stairs. As they climbed flight after flight, the Aldens told Miss Thompson the whole story about finding the deed in the old notebooks.

"Do you think you can help us?" Jessie asked when they finally reached the Land Records Room.

"If the deed is signed and stamped with the state seal, then all we need to do is make a copy and file it with Mr. Tully, the Land Records Clerk. Now don't worry if he seems a bit gruff. He likes to keep a close watch on the documents in the Records Room. And he's always a bit grumpy right before lunch."

"Me, too," Benny said.

Everyone's laughter bounced off the marble walls and floors when they went into the

Land Records Room. This did not please the annoyed-looking man who came over to the Aldens.

"What can I do for you, Miss Thompson?" the man asked. "I hope it's not too complicated. On Fridays, we lock up at twelve sharp, and it's ten of already."

"This is the Alden family, and they'd like us to find information about a fifty-year-old deed they discovered in Greenfield."

"Greenfield? What in heaven's name is going on in Greenfield?" Mr. Tully said in a loud voice. "Is someone putting up skyscrapers or something? Some employees of a demolition company were in just about an hour ago, asking about some Greenfield property, and I told 'em what I always tell 'em. They have to wait until Wednesday before their bid goes through, just in case a deed turns up by Tuesday. I sent them packing just like that pesky old woman who was here a few days ago, asking about the same darn land in Greenfield."

Henry stepped up to Mr. Tully. "Was it a Miss Newcombe?"

Mr. Tully thought for a minute. "I don't ask their names, young man, unless they have something official to show me. I can't help anyone without a piece of paper, and all this woman had was a lot of old stories. Why, I'd never get a day's work done if I spent time with these folks always coming in here with their stories." Mr. Tully looked at the Aldens and Miss Thompson as if they were trespassing on his private property.

"But we — " Jessie began.

"The Aldens do have — " Miss Thompson started to say, but Mr. Tully wanted to set everyone straight.

"This elderly woman seemed to think I could stop developers from building on some land she says might be hers. Why, I could say I owned the Grand Canyon, but without a deed, I certainly wouldn't get too far, now would I?"

"No, you wouldn't," Violet said in a quiet but sure voice. "But we do have a deed, Mr. Tully."

"That's quite impossible," Mr. Tully said.

"There was never a deed on that land, so it came to the state when the last owner of record died. Anybody can buy it once fifty years have passed after the owner's death, and that anniversary is Tuesday, just four days from now. The Wolf Demolition Company has already put in a preliminary bid, and after that they can buy the land fair and square." Mr. Tully paused and stared at the Aldens. "Unless, of course, someone shows up with a valid deed."

Henry stood tall. "You will find that *this* deed proves Miss Newcombe owns the land."

Mr. Tully raised an eyebrow. "Let me see that. Hmm. Hmm," he kept saying as he read the old document.

"Is this deed still good?" Henry asked.

"Good as the day it was signed," Mr. Tully said. "Now why this Jacob Kisco didn't file it, I don't know. Probably one of these old farmers who kept everything hidden under his mattress, I suppose, and didn't tell anyone about it."

Benny just couldn't stay still. "I found it,

Mr. Tully, but not under a mattress. It was hidden in a book stuck between two boards in a toolshed."

Mr. Tully could hardly stand this. "There you go. A toolshed! Fifty years ago this capitol was standing here same as now. Not to mention the Greenfield Town Hall. The old woman said there wasn't a thing filed there, either. Too bad she didn't check the toolshed! Well, here's the proof she needed right here."

The Aldens jumped up and down. Jessie almost hugged Mr. Tully, but she hugged her grandfather instead.

"The search paid off," Mr. Alden said. "You know, Mr. Tully, I've never known my grandchildren to give up on finding what they wanted."

Mr. Tully coughed a few times to quiet everyone down. "I wouldn't celebrate just yet," he said gruffly.

Jessie's voice was squeaky. "Why can't we celebrate?"

"The name on this deed is Silas Newcombe," Mr. Tully said. "That's a man's name, not the name of that woman. For all we know, Silas Newcombe could still be alive."

"It's Miss Newcombe's father," Henry said. "He died a long time ago."

Mr. Tully's face didn't change. "Well, how does anyone know he left the property to the woman who was here the other day? She would have to produce a will saying that the property was left to her. No will, no land."

The Aldens' hopes fell again. They not only didn't have a will, they didn't even have Miss Newcombe.

"We'll talk to her," Jessie said. She looked Mr. Tully in the eye. "And after we do, we'll be back with her father's will."

"You've only got until Tuesday, young lady," Mr. Tully said. "Otherwise, that Wolf Demolition Company can buy the land."

Everyone left the Land Records Office quietly before Mr. Tully could give them any more bad news.

"I'm sorry Mr. Tully wasn't more polite," Miss Thompson said. She put an arm around

Jessie's shoulder. "But the main thing is that the deed proves the property belongs to Miss Newcombe's family. All you have to do is get the will from her. She must be back in Greenfield by now."

Henry spoke up. "*If* she even went back to Greenfield. You see, these men from the demolition company seem to have frightened her away. That's what we think."

Miss Thompson stopped on the step where she was standing. "I see," she said softly. "That is a problem. As Mr. Tully said, time is running out. On Wednesday, this deed won't be any good. I'm afraid Mr. Tully is correct. The developers have a perfect right to buy the land from the state when the fifty-year anniversary of Jacob Kisco's death has passed."

The Aldens didn't speak the rest of the way down the winding stairs. No one had to. They were all thinking the same thing. Where was Miss Newcombe? She just *had* to be found.

CHAPTER 8

Lost and Found

The Aldens spent the next two days searching everywhere in Greenfield for Miss Newcombe.

On Monday, as everyone walked to the Greenfield Animal Shelter to help out and pick up supplies, Violet said, "Maybe she just didn't come back from the capital after she talked to Mr. Tully. Surely someone in town would have seen her by now if she had returned."

Henry, Jessie, and Benny didn't want to say out loud what they were thinking. Violet was probably right. Miss Newcombe didn't know they had the deed to her land. Maybe she was too discouraged or frightened to return to Greenfield.

Jessie spoke quietly. "I guess we'll just have to tell Dr. Scott today that we haven't had any luck so far."

They didn't have to tell Dr. Scott anything. She could see by everyone's faces they hadn't found Miss Newcombe.

"There's still the rest of today," Dr. Scott told Jessie, Violet, and Benny when they arrived at the shelter.

But Dr. Scott was upset, too. While the Aldens had to find Miss Newcombe, Dr. Scott still hadn't located the shelter's founder. Like the Aldens, she had very little time left. The two weeks were almost up.

Violet and Jessie spent the morning making phone calls to see if anyone in Greenfield wanted to adopt any animals from the shelter.

"We only found two homes," Jessie told Dr. Scott when she came back later to check on their progress.

"Why don't you girls make the rest of the calls from home? I have some volunteers coming in this afternoon," Dr. Scott told Jessie and Violet.

Just then, Henry came by. They could see by his excited face that he had some news.

"Mr. Knapp, the taxi driver, came into the store today," he began. "He said Miss Newcombe came in on the train just this morning. He dropped her off at the gate to her house! Let's go there right now."

"That's wonderful news, Henry," Dr. Scott said. She picked up the phone and dialed a number. After a long time, she hung up. "No answer. I thought I might find her home at last, but no one answered the phone."

"That's not going to stop us," Jessie said. "We'll go to Miss Newcombe's anyway."

"Good luck!" Dr. Scott said when the Aldens left the shelter. "Give me a call later on and let me know what happens."

The Aldens walked as quickly as they could to Fox Den Road. Henry broke into a run when they neared the Newcombe house. When the others caught up, they found Henry shaking the locked gate.

"Open up! Open up!" he called through the bars.

"It's no use, Henry," Jessie said. "No one's there. The truck is gone. All the windows are closed."

"Did Mr. Knapp say if he drove Miss Newcombe right up to the house?" Violet asked. "Did he see her go inside?"

Henry shook his head. "He told me she didn't want to keep him waiting while she unlocked the gate. He drove off before she opened it."

Jessie looked down at the ground. "Maybe she never got inside the gate."

Everyone walked the rest of the way home without saying a word. This was the closest they'd come to finding Miss Newcombe. But they had missed her.

Mrs. McGregor's good chicken dinner and Grandfather's encouraging words didn't help the children feel any better. This looked like one mystery that the Aldens weren't going to solve after all.

After dinner, they went about their boxcar chores in silence. Jessie cleaned the cages while Violet moved the cats and dogs into the boxcar for the night. Benny checked that all the water dishes were filled so none of the strays would be thirsty during the night.

Violet was especially sad. What had happened to Miss Newcombe? What would happen to her nice pets? How would they find homes for all the animals they had? All this worry kept Violet awake long after the rest of the family had fallen asleep.

Suddenly she heard the long, low sound of a heavy door being pushed.

"The boxcar!" she cried. She jumped from her bed and went to the window.

The moon was high above the Aldens' yard now. In the moonlight, Violet saw a gray-haired woman step inside the boxcar. "What is Mrs. McGregor doing out there this late?" she said to herself. She put on her robe, then tiptoed downstairs. Watch was at the back door, growling in a low voice.

"No need to growl, Watch," Violet whispered to the dog. "It's just Mrs. McGregor."

In the moonlight Violet found her way easily to the boxcar. When she was about ten feet away, she could hear a dog's tail thumping against the metal walls of the boxcar. All the dogs were yipping with excitement.

Violet knew those sounds very well. They were *not* frightened or unhappy sounds. These were the same happy cries the animals made when the Aldens came to visit, pet, or feed them. Somebody they liked very much was in the boxcar!

"Ah, Patches, you lovely, sweet thing," someone was saying inside. "I knew this was the right place for you."

Lad made an eager yelp.

"And you, too, Lad," the voice continued.

When Violet's eyes adjusted to the darkness, she saw a white-haired woman sitting down on an empty food crate. The woman was surrounded by Lad, the white dog, Patches, and a cat. They were all licking her and rubbing against her ankles.

"Excuse me," Violet said.

The woman jumped. In the moonlight, Violet saw the woman's eyes flash with fright.

"I'm sorry," Violet said softly. "I heard the door of the boxcar opening. I was worried about the animals." Violet paused. She didn't want to frighten the woman away by stepping inside.

"It's okay, Lad. Sit," the woman said, taking the dog's front paws off her lap.

"Lad?" Violet asked. "You know this dog?"

The woman stood up. She was hardly taller than Violet. She smoothed her dress and twisted a ring on her finger. "Many of the animals in here were mine," she began. "I left them here in your safekeeping."

Violet waited a long time before she said anything. "Then you must be Miss Newcombe."

"Yes. Clara Newcombe. I heard about your love of animals from Dr. Scott. And I knew your grandfather's family long ago. When I had to leave my animals, I knew they would have a good home here."

"You brought all these animals here?" Violet asked.

The woman stroked Patches on her forehead. "Yes, I left Patches here a week and a half ago and the other animals at good homes around town, but some of them ran away and tried to get back home. Late the other night, I saw Lady wandering around Greenfield, so I brought her here, too. As for Lad and Midnight, the cat, I don't know how they came to be here, but I'm glad they are. Lad and Lady are from the same litter."

Violet stroked Lad's floppy ear. "At first we called him Fred. I mean the people who found him did. A woman and her little boy saw him wandering around in the parking lot of their apartment building. A farmer who says he knows you brought Midnight to the Greenfield Animal Shelter. We took her because the shelter has to close."

When Violet said that, the woman sat down. "Yes, the shelter. I know all about the shelter closing," she said. She looked up at Violet. "That's why I didn't bring my animals there."

"You must come into our house," Violet said gently. "It's chilly out here." Violet led the animals back to their cages and helped the woman down from the boxcar. "Don't worry. Your pets are safe here tonight."

As they walked to the house, they saw the kitchen light go on. When Violet opened the back door, there was Henry, yawning and squinting. Not too far behind was a sleepy Jessie and a sleepy Benny. Mr. Alden, who did not look the least bit sleepy, had come downstairs, too. Watch, who often growled at strangers, did not growl at Miss Newcombe now. He seemed to like this woman without even knowing who she was.

"This is Miss Newcombe. Miss Newcombe, these are my brothers, Henry and Benny. That's Jessie. And, of course, you know who my grandfather is."

Mr. Alden pulled out a chair for Miss Newcombe. "Hello, Clara. It's been many years."

The tired woman sank into the chair. "Yes, too many, James. I've kept to myself so long."

Jessie was at the sink filling the kettle. "Let me get you some tea," she said.

"Miss Newcombe came to see Patches and Lad," Violet announced. "The new dog is called Lady, and she's Lad's sister."

Mr. Alden reached a hand out to Miss Newcombe. "My grandchildren have been searching for you for nearly two weeks. I know you like to keep to yourself, Clara, so perhaps you didn't want to be found. But they may have some special news for you."

Benny opened his mouth to speak, but whatever words he was going to say turned into a big yawn.

Jessie ran into the den and came back. In her hand was the farmer's black notebook with the deed tucked inside. "Here," she said, unfolding the yellowed paper. "Read this. We think this is an important piece of paper about your land."

The old woman looked less frightened now in the warm, well-lit kitchen. Who could be afraid of these kind faces?

The woman read the paper once, then seemed to read it again. Finally she looked up at everyone. "You don't know how important this deed is."

"Ah, but they do," Mr. Alden said. "My grandchildren have been investigating some strange goings-on at your house. They have reason to believe a demolition company has got hold of your property. They intend to develop it if they can buy it for good when it comes up for sale tomorrow."

The woman nodded her head up and down. "How right they are. You see, years ago this property belonged to Jacob Kisco. Back then my father rented from him the house, the two barns, and some meadows for the price of the milk, eggs, butter, and cheese he got from our herd of cows. Mr. Kisco always said he had made arrangements to leave the land to our family when he died, but he never gave my father the deed."

Mr. Alden sat down at the table a few feet across from Miss Newcombe. "But everyone in Greenfield always thought the land belonged to your family, Clara."

Miss Newcombe lowered her eyes and twisted the lace handkerchief in her hands.

She didn't speak for a long time. When she finally did, her voice was shaky. "Yes, I know that's what people thought. You see, my father only planned to stay on the property until the state came to claim it. But they never sent anyone, so Father stayed there. After he died, I stayed on, too."

"Miss Newcombe," Henry said softly. "Was the Greenfield Animal Shelter part of Mr. Kisco's land at the time that he died?"

Miss Newcombe's soft blue eyes looked frightened again, and she could hardly hold her cup of tea. "I guess I have to tell the other part of the story. You see, I felt so guilty about staying on land that probably belonged to the state, I offered the state use of some of the property when they wanted to open an animal shelter in these parts. At the same time, I wanted to protect my father's good name, so I kept the Newcombe name out in case the truth ever came out."

"So *you're* the founder!" Jessie cried out.

"Yes, I am," Miss Newcombe said. "I didn't want to let anyone know because I worried that someone would take away the land someday. Now someone has."

Violet patted Miss Newcombe's hand to make her feel better. Jessie refilled her cup.

"I love animals, you know. I fully expected to make a bid on the land when fifty years had passed after Mr. Kisco's death. But then these terrible men showed up."

Now Benny was awake. "With the bad, rusty truck that's always following us," he told Miss Newcombe. "They called our house with scary voices, and stole Grandfather's gas, and put a bad note in Jessie's newspapers."

She patted Benny's hand. "Yes, Benny. Those men scared me, too. They told me they had already bought the land and I had to leave. They ordered me to close down the shelter. I wondered whether there was any way to stop this from happening, so I went up to the capital to check old property records. I didn't want anyone to know what had happened, so I left Greenfield quietly."

"Is that when you sent your pets to different families?" Jessie asked.

"Yes. I knew from my friend, Dr. Scott,

that your family liked animals, so I dropped Patches off one night. I left animals at other places around town. I was in such a state, I didn't have time to write notes to everyone or even check the animal tags and such. And, of course, I see some of the pets wandered away from where I left them and tried to find their way home again."

Jessie brought out some of Mrs. McGregor's coffee cake and set it in front of the woman. "Where have you been staying all this time?" she asked.

"Different places. I found a small room at the state capital so I could see some lawyers and visit the Land Records Office. That turned out to be a disappointing trip."

"I bet Mr. Tully thought you were bothering him," Benny said.

Miss Newcombe smiled a bit. "Yes, I'm afraid such a busy man didn't have much time for someone with no papers or proof that the land belonged to my father, who left it to me in his will."

"The will!" Henry cried. "Do you have a will?"

"Yes, of course," Miss Newcombe said. "I was my father's only child, and he left everything to me, including the land he was sure Mr. Kisco had left him."

"The will is all you need," Mr. Alden explained. "That and this deed. You stay here with us tonight. Then tomorrow I'll drive up to the capital and file this deed before the deadline. You'll be back in your own home by tomorrow afternoon."

The old woman took a long sip of tea to calm herself. "Do you really think so?"

"Yes, indeed!" Benny said loudly. "Yes, indeed."

CHAPTER 9

Moving Day

"Shh. Quiet, Watch," Jessie whispered when she heard Watch growling. "It's too early to get up."

Watch did not agree with Jessie and growled long and low. When Jessie's eyes adjusted to the darkness, she saw Watch looking out the bedroom window over the driveway. Jessie was wide awake now and went to the window, too.

She stroked Watch's alert ears. "What is it, boy?"

Jessie didn't really need Watch's answer.

Under the streetlamp, she could see the out-
lines of a pickup truck parked on the street.
Whoever was in the car was smoking and
flicking ashes out the window every few
minutes.

"I don't know if that's the truck, but I'm
not taking any chances," Jessie told Watch.

She tiptoed down the hall to the phone
table and dialed the Greenfield Police De-
partment. "Hello, hello, this is Jessie Alden,"
she whispered into the phone. "I'm calling
to report a suspicious . . . oh, hello, Officer
Lawler. Yes, I know it's early, but that's why
I'm calling. There's a truck parked in front
of my grandfather's house, and I think there
might be some men in it who've been bothering Miss Newcombe on Fox Den Road and
my family, too. Could a policeman drive by
our house just in case they're going to make
trouble? Yes, thank you."

"Whew," Jessie said when she put down
the phone.

"What are you whewing about?" Henry
said, making Jessie practically jump out of
her robe. "It's five o'clock in the morning."

"I know. That's why I just called Officer Lawler at the police station to check on that suspicious truck out there. See," she whispered. "Careful, don't get in front of the window. They might see you."

Henry pulled aside the curtain carefully and stood off to the side. "Hey, they're getting out and walking toward Grandfather's car. I'm going out there."

When Henry put his hand on the lightswitch, Jessie stopped him. "Don't do that. Maybe this time we can catch them doing something while they think we're asleep. Officer Lawler said he was leaving right away."

Henry rubbed his eyes. "You're right."

Jessie and Henry tiptoed downstairs. The kitchen window was open a few inches to let in the night air. Henry and Jessie crouched down near the sink where they couldn't be seen but right where they could hear the men whispering to each other.

"Four bum tires ought to do the trick," one voice said. "Sam, where's that knife you always carry?"

Jessie grabbed Henry's arm. "Oh, no, I

think they're going to slash the tires so we can't use Grandfather's car today!"

Jessie and Henry were listening so hard to make out what the men were saying, they didn't hear Officer Lawler's cruiser pull up.

"Hands behind your back!" a deep voice shouted.

Henry and Jessie heard the men's knife clatter to the driveway. That's when the kitchen lights went on.

"Heavens, me, why are you both huddled by the sink?" Mrs. McGregor asked.

Benny came in next, carrying his blanket, followed by Violet, who was blinking hard and trying to figure out what the commotion was all about.

"My goodness," Mr. Alden said when he came into the kitchen to find five people all up at this very early hour. "I'm not leaving for the capital for hours. I hope you'll all quietly go back to bed before we wake up Miss Newcombe."

"But Grandfather — " Jessie began.

"You see, the police are — "

"My word, there's the doorbell!" Mrs.

McGregor said. "I must be dreaming. That's the only explanation for why I'm down in this chilly kitchen with everyone instead of in my nice warm bed."

Mr. Alden led the way to the front hall and opened the door. "Why, Officer Lawler, you're the last person I expected to see on my porch at this hour."

"That may be, Mr. Alden," the policeman said, "but one of your quick-thinking grand-children helped me catch three vandals who were trying to slash your tires. I'm afraid they did some damage to one of them, but the other tires are fine."

Mr. Alden put his arm around Jessie. "I'll bet this is our detective. She's the only one who looks wide awake enough to find the phone, let alone dial the right number for the police station."

Jessie shivered, but she felt warm inside. "Are those men from the Wolf Demolition Company, Officer Lawler?"

The policeman checked his notepad. "That's a good name for what they are — wolves who hunt in the night. But I've got them caged, all right. They're locked up in the backseat of my cruiser. So if you'll file a complaint later today, we can register the arrest." Officer Lawler tipped his cap. "Good-night, or maybe I should say good-morning."

"I'd better get some coffee perking," Mrs. McGregor said. "I know you've all got a busy day ahead."

An hour later, everyone, including Miss Newcombe, was wide awake, dressed, and ready to get on with that busy day.

"Benny and I changed the bad tire, Grand-father," Henry said. "I started the engine for a minute, and the gas gauge needle is on full."

Mr. Alden said, "I'm sorry not to have my backseat drivers on this trip, but I know you'll want to get the animal shelter business straightened out now that Miss Newcombe is back. And, Clara, I imagine you'll want to phone Dr. Scott."

Miss Newcombe took Mr. Alden's hand into hers. "Thank you, James. I feel like a new person today after the first restful sleep I've had in two weeks. Knowing I can go back to my own home, well, it means everything to me."

"You can thank my grandchildren for that, Clara," Mr. Alden said. He patted his suit pocket. "Well, the deed is in here, and I'll pick up the will from your lawyer on the way out of town. So we're all set."

After everyone waved off Mr. Alden, they went out to the boxcar to check on the animals.

Miss Newcombe's step was young and lively this morning. "I can hardly wait to see my dear cats curled on their favorite chairs. And I know it will cheer me to see Lad and Lady running in the meadows and through the woods. Not that they haven't loved your boxcar," the elderly lady told the Aldens when they peeked into the boxcar. "All of you did a wonderful job making a home for them."

Violet's thank-you could hardly be heard. She was blinking back tears.

Miss Newcombe handed her a white hanky. "I know just how you feel, dear. It will be hard to part from your new friends.

That's why I want you to come visit me whenever you want. I think I'll start getting newspaper delivery again to keep up with the news — news of the Aldens!"

This made even Violet laugh, and everyone was still laughing when Dr. Scott drove up in her station wagon to pick up Miss Newcombe and her pets.

She gave Miss Newcombe a huge hug. "Why, Clara Newcombe! Imagine keeping a secret from me all these years. I must be better at figuring out animals than people not to guess that you were the founder of the Greenfield Animal Shelter."

Miss Newcombe's cheeks got pinker than ever. "That's all right, Mary. There were reasons I was so secretive, but now, thanks to all of you, I don't have to be."

"Is it time?" Henry asked in a quieter voice than usual.

Miss Newcombe smiled. "You can get the leashes and cages for the ride home."

Henry called Miss Newcombe's two dogs. "Here, Lad. Come here, Lady."

The dogs stood nice and still while Henry

fastened on their leashes. He opened the back of Dr. Scott's station wagon and let the dogs in. Up front, he cleared some space for two cat carriers. "We should be able to fit Patches and Midnight up here, and the gray cat in a cage in back."

Violet slid the gray cat's cage across the backseat where there was just enough room for it.

Miss Newcombe looked puzzled. "Why are you giving me this cat?" she asked.

Violet checked inside the carrier to make sure she had the right animal. "Isn't she yours? She was in the boxcar the night you brought Lady here, remember? That rainy night?"

Miss Newcombe shook her head. "Why, I found that cat wandering outside the boxcar that night. I thought she lived in the boxcar already and had just gotten out. So I put her in an empty cage. She isn't mine."

At this news, Violet broke into a big smile. "Maybe we'll get to keep one of the strays, after all. Now that the Greenfield Animal Shelter can stay open, our boxcar will be practically empty." She opened the cage and lifted the pretty gray Persian in her arms. "And I do like this fluffy cat."

Unlike Patches and Midnight, the gray cat was a shy one and never went too far from the boxcar or from people.

"She's such a frightened one, isn't she?" Violet asked. "I'd hoped that with the other cats gone, she would look around the yard a bit more."

"She must have been an indoor cat, she's so shy of every little thing," Henry told his sister.

"And every big thing," Benny said. He pointed to Watch, who was standing nearby and not a bit pleased with all the attention this ball of fur was getting.

The gray cat looked terrified of Watch.

Violet stroked the frightened Persian. "Poor cat. That gives me an idea. I know someone who would like you very much," she said before she ran into the house.

Everyone looked puzzled, especially Benny. "Where does Violet want to send this cat, Jessie?"

Benny didn't have to wait long for an answer. Violet was back in no time. "It's all set," she announced. "I'm sending this cat to the O'Connors, you know, the mother and the little boy who found Lad wandering around near their apartment. Jeffrey wanted a pet so much, especially a nice cat. And this is a nice cat! So I called the number they gave me when we met them and told them all about this cat. They'll be over right away to pick her up."

"Then we'd better pick her up," Benny said. He bent down to catch the Persian. "Animals always run away just when you need them."

Miss Newcombe's eyes were twinkling. "Sometimes people run away when you need them, too!"

"But we always find them," Benny said.

"I *am* glad you found me," Miss Newcombe said. "I won't run away again. I'll be nearby with my dear pets and my dear new friends!"

GERTRUDE CHANDLER WARNER discovered when she was teaching that many readers who like an exciting story could find no books that were both easy and fun to read. She decided to try to meet this need, and her first book, *The Boxcar Children*, quickly proved she had succeeded.

Miss Warner drew on her own experiences to write the mystery. As a child she spent hours watching trains go by on the tracks opposite her family home. She often dreamed about what it would be like to set up housekeeping in a caboose or freight car — the situation the Alden children find themselves in.

When Miss Warner received requests for more adventures involving Henry, Jessie, Violet, and Benny Alden, she began additional stories. In each, she chose a special setting and introduced unusual or eccentric characters who liked the unpredictable.

While the mystery element is central to each of Miss Warner's books, she never thought of them as strictly juvenile mysteries. She liked to stress the Aldens' independence and resourcefulness and their solid New England devotion to using up and making do. The Aldens go about most of their adventures with as little adult supervision as possible — something else that delights young readers.

Miss Warner lived in Putnam, Connecticut, until her death in 1979. During her lifetime, she received hundreds of letters from girls and boys telling her how much they liked her books.